CHAPTER ONE

THIS IS THE RAINFOREST, ON A MORNING WITHOUT RAIN.

SAVING SORYA

CHANG AND THE SUN BEAR

WRITTEN BY **TRANG NGUYEN**

ILLUSTRATED BY **JEET ZDUNG**

DIAL BOOKS FOR YOUNG READERS

TO DAISY, LINH ĐAN,
AND ALL YOUNG
ANIMAL LOVERS
EVERYWHERE.

HELLO READERS,

MY NAME IS TRANG, AND I AM A VIETNAMESE WILDLIFE CONSERVATIONIST. *SAVING SORYA: CHANG AND THE SUN BEAR* IS THE STORY OF CHANG, A LITTLE GIRL WITH A HUGE DREAM TO PROTECT AND CONSERVE WILD ANIMALS WHO ARE BEING PUSHED TOWARD EXTINCTION BY HUMANS. CHANG WORKS HARD TO FOLLOW HER DREAMS, AND SHE IGNORES PEOPLE WHO SAY WILDLIFE CONSERVATION IS NOT A GOOD CAREER FOR HER.

WHEN CHANG MEETS SORYA, A SMALL AND TIMID SUN BEAR, CHANG DECIDES SHE WILL DO EVERYTHING SHE CAN TO RETURN SORYA TO THE RAINFOREST. THIS IS A STORY INSPIRED BY REAL CHARACTERS AND EVENTS: CHANG IS BASED ON ME. MY LIFE CHANGED WHEN I ACCIDENTALLY WITNESSED A MOON BEAR WHOSE BILE WAS BEING EXTRACTED. AT THAT MOMENT, I DECIDED THERE WAS NOTHING ELSE I WANTED TO DO MORE THAN BECOME A CONSERVATIONIST AND CREATE A BETTER, SAFER WORLD FOR WILD ANIMALS.

SORYA IS A REAL SUN BEAR WHO WAS RESCUED FROM THE ILLEGAL BEAR TRADE BY A WONDERFUL ORGANIZATION IN SOUTHEAST ASIA CALLED FREE THE BEARS. BUT HER JOURNEY IN THIS BOOK IS BASED ON THE STORY OF A MOON BEAR NAMED POLA. POLA WAS RESCUED IN 2008 AND REINTRODUCED TO THE WILD.

IN READING THIS STORY, YOU'LL LEARN MORE ABOUT AN AMAZING CREATURE--THE SUN BEAR--AND ITS IMPORTANT ROLE IN THE FOREST, AS WELL AS THE LIFE-SAVING CONSERVATION WORK THAT'S HAPPENING TO PROTECT THESE ANIMALS AND THEIR HOMES. I HOPE THIS STORY GIVES YOU THE ENCOURAGEMENT AND INSPIRATION TO FOLLOW YOUR OWN DREAMS, WHATEVER THEY MAY BE, AND TO NEVER GIVE UP.

TRANG

IT IS FULL OF WILD PLANTS AND ANIMALS.

OOF!

SORYA, NO!

BAD BEAR, SORYA!

SNIFF!
SLURP!

OH, SORYA--MY NOTEBOOK'S ALL WET!

GRRR

THIS IS SORYA, A LOVELY LITTLE SUN BEAR.

WHAT ARE YOU SNIFFING AT?

YOU ARE NOT A DOG!

SLURP

YOU'RE A WILD BEAR, REMEMBER?

SHE WAS CAPTURED AND SENT TO A BEAR BILE FARM WHEN SHE WAS A BABY.

GO LOOK FOR FOOD YOURSELF!

HOW ARE YOU GOING TO LIVE IN THE FOREST IF YOU KEEP WAITING FOR ME TO FEED YOU?

MY JOB IS TO BRING HER BACK TO THE FOREST AND TEACH HER HOW TO LIVE ON HER OWN.

GRRR

EEK!

A TOAD

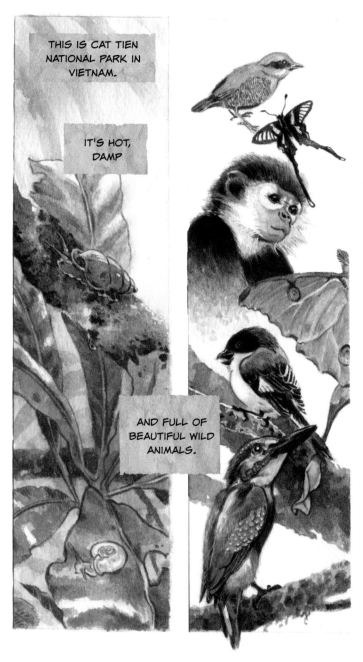

THIS IS CAT TIEN NATIONAL PARK IN VIETNAM.

IT'S HOT, DAMP

AND FULL OF BEAUTIFUL WILD ANIMALS.

IT IS ALSO HOME TO VICIOUS MOSQUITOES.

THEY CAN CAUSE A DEADLY DISEASE CALLED MALARIA.

BUT LEECHES ARE EVEN WORSE. THEY ARE BLOOD-SUCKERS.

LEECHES CRAWL...

EVERY-WHERE!

My natural insect repellent scares the mosquitoes and leeches off.

organic lime and lemongrass

apply here

and here

FLICK...

I ALSO USE A STICK TO FLICK THE LEECHES AWAY.

CRACK!

SCRATCH...

SNIFF...

SCRATCH...

SNIFF...

SLURP!

PANT PANT!

The sun is shining, a day without mosquitoes.

Sorya has learned to find honey all by herself!

Chang

A WONDERFUL MORNING!

17

CHAPTER TWO

I'VE WANTED TO BECOME A CONSERVATIONIST SINCE I WAS EIGHT YEARS OLD. IT ALL BEGAN WHEN I WAS WALKING BACK FROM SCHOOL WITH A FRIEND...

WE HEARD A TERRIBLE NOISE COMING FROM INSIDE A HOUSE.

UHH
UHH
UHH

WE CREPT CLOSER. TO OUR SURPRISE, WE COULD HEAR VOICES.

?

EWW! WHAT'S THAT SMELL?!

WE PEERED INSIDE AND SAW SOMETHING AWFUL.

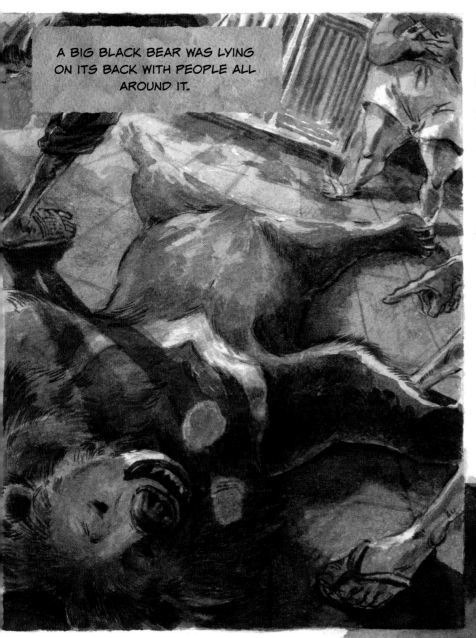

A BIG BLACK BEAR WAS LYING ON ITS BACK WITH PEOPLE ALL AROUND IT.

THE TERRIBLE SOUND WE HAD HEARD EARLIER WAS THE BEAR CRYING.

UHH

A MAN WAS STANDING ABOVE IT HOLDING A GIANT NEEDLE.

NOOOOO!

WE WERE SO FRIGHTENED WE RAN AWAY.

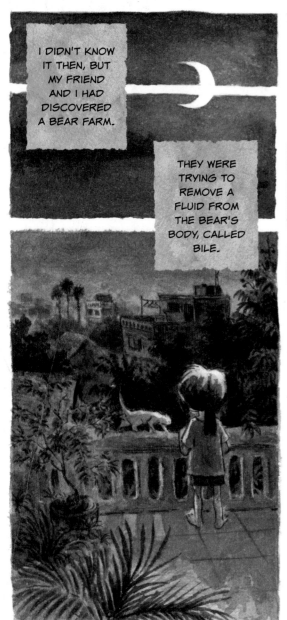

I DIDN'T KNOW IT THEN, BUT MY FRIEND AND I HAD DISCOVERED A BEAR FARM.

THEY WERE TRYING TO REMOVE A FLUID FROM THE BEAR'S BODY, CALLED BILE.

BEAR BILE HAS BEEN USED IN MEDICINE FOR THOUSANDS OF YEARS.

BUT NOW WE HAVE MEDICINE THAT DOESN'T USE IT, AND DOESN'T HURT BEARS.

THAT NIGHT I MADE A PROMISE TO MYSELF. I WOULD NOT LET HUMANS ABUSE BEARS, OR ANY OTHER WILD ANIMALS, IF I COULD STOP THEM.

SO, THE VERY NEXT DAY,
I DECIDED TO BECOME A
WILDLIFE CONSERVATIONIST.

I HAD HEARD
ABOUT
WILDLIFE
CONSERVATIONISTS
ON TV.
THEY ARE
PEOPLE WHO
PROTECT NATURE ALL
OVER THE WORLD--
IN DESERTS, NEAR
OCEANS, AND EVEN
INSIDE CAVES.

THAT'S WHEN I
REALIZED:
I COULD
PROTECT THE
RAINFOREST
NEAR MY HOME!

NOTHING'S GOING TO STOP ME!

WELL, THERE WAS ONE THING STOPPING ME... ALL THE BOOKS I FOUND ABOUT CONSERVATION WERE IN **ENGLISH!**

GRRR! I DON'T UNDERSTAND ANYTHING!

MY ENGLISH IS TERRIBLE.

PEOPLE ALSO HAD A LOT TO SAY ABOUT MY PLAN...

HOW CAN A GIRL LIKE YOU WORK IN THE FOREST?

HA HA HA, SUCH A KID DREAM.

YOU SHOULD BE REALISTIC. BE A TEACHER OR AN ACCOUNTANT!

ONLY WESTERNERS CAN BE CONSERVATIONISTS. THEY HAVE TIME AND MONEY.

YOU CAN'T EVEN TAKE CARE OF YOURSELF; HOW CAN YOU PROTECT WILD ANIMALS?

A GIRL LIKE YOU SHOULD CONCENTRATE ON SCHOOL, THEN GET MARRIED WHEN YOU GROW UP.

DON'T BE RIDICULOUS!

PEOPLE DON'T DO THAT IN VIETNAM!

AND MY GENDER...

GIRLS ARE SO WEAK! THERE IS NO WAY YOU CAN PROTECT WILD ANIMALS.

PANT PANT PANT PANT PANT PANT

I WANT TO BE A VOLUNTEER AT YOUR ORGANIZATION.

THANK YOU, BUT YOU ARE SO SMALL.

ONLY EIGHT YEARS OLD!

AND EVEN MY AGE. NO ONE WOULD HIRE ME.

IT WAS AMAZING WORKING AS AN ANIMAL-RESCUE VOLUNTEER IN CAT TIEN NATIONAL PARK. I MADE FRIENDS WITH ANIMAL LOVERS FROM ALL OVER THE WORLD AND LEARNED A LOT ABOUT CONSERVATION.

WILDLIFE RESCUE AND CONSERVATION CENTER

TOGETHER WE PREPARED FOOD FOR ALL THE CREATURES LIVING THERE. THEY WERE OFTEN SICK AND INJURED.

WE CLEANED UP BEAR POOP AND MADE HAMMOCKS FOR THE BEARS TO USE.

THE ANIMALS WERE RESCUED FROM POACHERS --PEOPLE WHO CAPTURE AND HURT WILD ANIMALS BEFORE THEY SELL THEM.

WE ALSO HELPED PANGOLINS-- ONE OF THE MOST ENDANGERED ANIMALS IN THE WORLD.

BUT I NEVER FORGOT THE BEAR I SAW ON THE FLOOR OF THAT BILE FARM.

SO I VOLUNTEERED AT FREE THE BEARS--AN ORGANIZATION THAT RESCUED BEARS FROM BILE FARMS ALL OVER SOUTHEAST ASIA.

THE POOR BEARS WERE FINALLY FREE FROM THEIR TERRIBLE, TINY CAGES.

FREE THE BEARS

CHAPTER THREE

ONE DAY, A TINY TWO-WEEK-OLD BEAR CUB ARRIVED AT THE CENTER.

HER NAME WAS **SORYA,** MEANING "SUN" IN VIETNAMESE.

SORYA WAS CAPTURED FROM A FOREST IN LAOS. WE DON'T KNOW WHAT HAPPENED TO HER MOTHER, BUT WE GUESSED THAT POACHERS HAD GOTTEN HER.

SORYA WAS VERY DIFFERENT FROM MISA.

THERE ARE TWO SPECIES OF BEARS IN VIETNAM:

THE MOON BEAR: THE SUN BEAR:

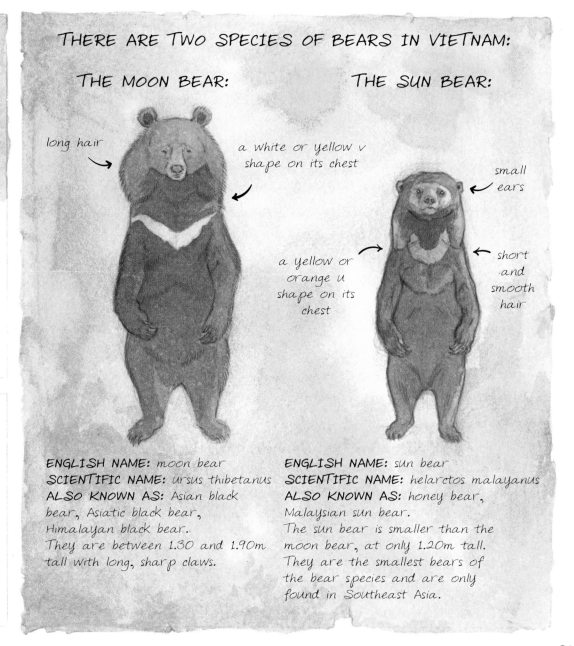

long hair

a white or yellow v shape on its chest

a yellow or orange u shape on its chest

small ears

short and smooth hair

ENGLISH NAME: *moon bear*
SCIENTIFIC NAME: *ursus thibetanus*
ALSO KNOWN AS: *Asian black bear, Asiatic black bear, Himalayan black bear.*
They are between 1.30 and 1.90m tall with long, sharp claws.

ENGLISH NAME: *sun bear*
SCIENTIFIC NAME: *helarctos malayanus*
ALSO KNOWN AS: *honey bear, Malaysian sun bear.*
The sun bear is smaller than the moon bear, at only 1.20m tall. They are the smallest bears of the bear species and are only found in Southeast Asia.

THERE ARE EIGHT SPECIES
OF BEARS IN THE WORLD:

PANDA

MOON BEAR

SLOTH BEAR

POLAR BEAR

SUN BEAR

SPECTACLED
BEAR

AMERICAN BLACK BEAR

BROWN
BEAR

GOOD CLIMBERS:
THEY SPEND MORE TIME IN TREES THAN ANY OTHER BEAR SPECIES.

OMNIVORES:
THEY EAT BOTH ANIMALS AND PLANTS --ANYTHING FROM EGGS, HONEY, FRUITS, AND ROOTS TO INSECTS, REPTILES, BIRDS, AND ANTS.

SUN BEARS ALSO LIKE COCONUTS! THEY USE THEIR STRONG CLAWS TO TEAR THE COCONUTS APART.

BIRDS MUST BE ABLE TO FLY!

AND BEARS MUST BE ABLE TO CLIMB!

AGILE FEET:
SHARP CLAWS CURVED LIKE HOOKS, AND THE BOTTOM OF THEIR PAWS DON'T HAVE FUR.

THEIR FEET POINT INWARD, SO THEY HAVE A VERY FUNNY WALK!

33

EVEN THOUGH ALL BEARS BELONG IN THE WILD, I LEARNED THAT NOT ALL BEARS, ONCE THEY ARE CAPTURED BY HUMANS, CAN RETURN.

LIKE MISA.

MISA IS OLD AND SICK. SHE HAS BEEN KEPT IN TINY CAGES FOR TOO LONG AND DOESN'T KNOW HOW TO FEND FOR HERSELF.

MISA MUST BE TAKEN CARE OF.

BEARS LIKE MISA LIVE IN CAPTIVITY
FOR THE REST OF THEIR LIVES.
BUT AT FREE THE BEARS, THEY ARE ABLE
TO LIVE IN A SMALL, PROTECTED PART
OF THE NATIONAL PARK, WHERE THEY
FEEL LIKE THEY ARE IN THE WILD.

SHE WAS SMALL, BUT YOUNG AND HEALTHY WHEN WE RESCUED HER.

SHE HAD A GOOD CHANCE OF LEARNING TO FEND FOR HERSELF AND RETURNING TO THE FOREST WHEN SHE WAS OLDER.

SINCE SORYA LOST HER MOTHER, I WAS IN CHARGE OF TEACHING HER SURVIVAL SKILLS, SUCH AS...

FORAGING AND HUNTING FOR FOOD,

FRESH WATER,

AND A SAFE PLACE TO SLEEP AT NIGHT.

LIKE SOME CUBS WITHOUT MOTHERS, SORYA ALSO DEVELOPED A HABIT OF SUCKING ON HER TOES AND FINGERS.

IT WAS CUTE AT FIRST, BUT EVERY TIME SORYA DID THIS...

SLURP! SUCK!

OH NO! YOUR PAWS ARE BLEEDING!

SHE'D BREAK THE SKIN AROUND HER TOENAILS AND HURT HERSELF.

Rescued bears often behave strangely.

Some walk back and forth, like they are still inside invisible cages.

Some are covered in scabs, from where they have rubbed their bodies on the bars of their cages.

Some of them don't have fur anymore because of stress or a skin condition that hasn't been treated in time.

Some shake their heads constantly.

These are all signs that some bears can't return to the wild. They've been suffering for too long, and wouldn't be able to take care of themselves.

THEIR BEHAVIOR WAS DUE TO MONTHS OR YEARS OF BEING KEPT IN TINY CAGES WHERE THEY COULD NOT MOVE OR STAND. HUMANS HAD BEEN CONSTANTLY EXTRACTING THEIR BILE, AND NOW THE BEARS COULDN'T FORGET THAT PAIN--OR THEIR FEAR.

THIS WAS SO TERRIBLE.

I WILL HELP SORYA TO RETURN TO THE WILD!

CHAPTER FOUR

AT THE BEAR RESCUE CENTER

IN THE EARLY MORNING...

WE PREPARED FOOD FOR BEARS,

HEY!

BUT OTHER ANIMALS CAME FOR THEIR SHARE!

COME ON, SORYA!

JUST A LITTLE HIGHER!

ALMOST THERE!

PANT!

YAY! YOU GOT IT, SORYA!

HA HA! YOU ARE SO CUTE.

EACH DAY I LEFT SORYA'S FOOD IN DIFFERENT PLACES SO SHE'D HAVE TO FIND IT HERSELF.

SORYA WAS GOOD AT FINDING HER MORNING BANANA.

?

BUT BULLIES TRIED TO TAKE IT FROM HER!

OH NO! THE OTHER BEAR GOT THE BANANA!

GRRRRR

TAKE IT BACK, SORYA.

BE BRAVE!

BUT SORYA WAS TOO SCARED.

I'M SORRY, CHANG. I DON'T THINK YOUR TRAINING WITH SORYA IS WORKING.

SHE'S WEAKER THAN THE OTHER BEARS. IF SHE CAN'T STAND UP FOR HERSELF, SHE'LL NEVER BE ABLE TO MAKE IT ON HER OWN.

THE NEXT FOREST WAS BEAUTIFUL.

I WAS VERY EXCITED. BUT THEN...

I DISCOVERED A DAM--A HUMAN-MADE BARRIER USED TO CONTROL WATER.

DURING THE RAINY SEASON, THE DAM WAS OPENED, ALLOWING WATER TO FLOOD THE FOREST.

MANY WILD ANIMALS DROWNED BECAUSE OF THESE FLOODS.

SORYA COULDN'T LIVE THERE.

THE FOURTH FOREST WASN'T A FOREST AT ALL.

IT WAS A CONSTRUCTION SITE, WHERE HOTELS, SHOPPING CENTERS, GOLF COURSES, AND OTHER BUILDINGS WERE BEING BUILT.

SORYA COULDN'T LIVE THERE EITHER.

WAS THERE ANYWHERE FOR HER TO LIVE?

IT WAS SO...

QUIET.

I WAS SURPRISED BECAUSE A LIVING FOREST IS USUALLY VERY NOISY, FILLED WITH THE SOUNDS OF WILDLIFE.

FINALLY, I FIGURED OUT WHY THERE WAS NO NOISE:

SNARE TRAPS.

I RAN AS FAST AS I COULD BACK TO THE CENTER TO GET HELP.

THE OTHER CONSERVATIONISTS AND I VISITED THE VILLAGE NEAR THE FOREST TO MEET THE LOCAL PEOPLE.

THEY TOLD US THAT POACHERS FROM OTHER PROVINCES CAME THERE TO HUNT ANIMALS...

AND SELL THEM IN THE CITIES.

MANY WILD ANIMALS
AND PLANTS ARE
THREATENED WITH
EXTINCTION DUE TO
HUMAN DEMAND.

SMALL
ANIMALS
LIKE
SQUIRRELS,
BIRDS, AND
LORISES ARE
CAUGHT AND
SOLD AS PETS,
OR KILLED
AND MADE INTO
PRODUCTS.

EVEN
PLANTS LIKE
ORCHIDS
HAVE BEEN
DISAPPEARING
FROM THE
FOREST.

FREE THE BEARS AND I ORGANIZED TRAINING AND WORKSHOPS FOR THE VILLAGERS.

WE GAVE THEM PROTECTIVE GEAR, LIKE FIELD SHOES AND CLOTHING.

FREE THE BEARS EVEN EMPLOYED THEM TO REMOVE SNARE TRAPS AND KEEP AN EYE ON THE FOREST.

WITHOUT SNARE TRAPS,

WILD ANIMALS STARTED
TO RETURN.

AND WHEN THE FOREST BEGAN TO FILL AGAIN
WITH THE SOUNDS OF WILDLIFE...

I KNEW SORYA COULD
LIVE THERE.

CHAPTER SIX

DURING THIS TIME, SORYA HAD GROWN UP.

SHE WAS MUCH BIGGER THAN SHE USED TO BE, AND COULD EVEN USE HER CLAWS TO BREAK OPEN COCONUTS, HER FAVORITE FOOD!

BEFORE, SORYA HAD BEEN TIMID, AND WAS CONSTANTLY BULLIED BY BIGGER BEARS. NOW, SHE COULD STAND UP FOR HERSELF, AND PROTECT HER FOOD AND SLEEPING NEST.

THERE WERE STILL THINGS FOR SORYA TO LEARN, BUT I KNEW SHE WAS READY FOR HER NEW HOME.

STAY STILL, SORYA. LET ME PUT THIS TRACKING COLLAR ON YOU.

THE COLLAR WOULD HELP US TRACK SORYA'S LOCATION.

UHH

DON'T BE SCARED, SORYA. YOU'RE ALMOST HOME!

ARE YOU OKAY?

RIBBIT

axlewood fruit

makha-tae tree

still so shy

Sorya loves swimming and playing in the water.

A rainy day

Sorya watches a bee on a crape myrtle flower.

She tries to eat a new plant now and then.

Wild bear cubs learn what is good to eat by smelling their mother's breath. But baby bears like Sorya, who were separated from their mothers, have to try everything. If it doesn't taste good, they spit it out.

Even though Sorya is getting used to the forest,

she still sleeps by me at night.

CROAKKK

CROOAAKK

ONE NIGHT, THE SOUND OF A FROG CAUGHT SORYA'S ATTENTION.

CROOAAKK

SORYA WAS HUNGRY.

SHE WANTED ME TO FEED HER, BUT I WAS TOO TIRED, SO I PRETENDED TO BE ASLEEP.

WHOOSH!!

BUT THEN...

THAT'S IT, SORYA! **COME ON!**

SORYA FOUND A REALLY BIG TERMITE NEST.

QUICKLY, SHE USED HER STRONG PAWS AND SHARP CLAWS TO DIG INTO IT.

AND STRETCHED HER LOOOOOONG TONGUE INSIDE.

(A SUN BEAR'S TONGUE CAN BE AS LONG AS 25cm!)

THAT DAY, SORYA PROVED THAT SHE WAS A REAL WILD BEAR, DOING THINGS SHE COULD NOT HAVE DONE BEFORE!

CHAPTER SEVEN

AND MET SOME AMAZING WILD ANIMALS ALONG THE WAY,

SUCH AS **GAURS.**

THE LOCAL PEOPLE CALL THEM MIN. THEY ARE SOME OF THE BIGGEST AND STRONGEST ANIMALS IN THE AREA.

THIS GAUR WAS VIGILANT! I KNEW I'D BETTER STAY AWAY FROM HIM.

SOMETIMES, SORYA GOT AHEAD OF ME, AND I HAD TO USE THE TRACKER ON HER COLLAR TO FIND HER.

SHE COULD MAKE HER WAY THROUGH THICK BAMBOO, BUT I COULDN'T.

OUCH!

SORYA HAD BECOME MUCH BRAVER, AND WAS STARTING TO EXPLORE BY HERSELF.

THE JOURNEY WAS TOUGH, BUT THE DISCOVERIES WE MADE TOGETHER WERE WORTH IT.

Sun bears like Sorya are called the "doctors" and "gardeners" of the rainforest. They make the forest healthier and help it in lots of ways.

For example, they eat lots of fruit and spread seeds through their poop!

They eat termites,

controlling pest populations.

From these seeds grow new plants.

Sun bears break up rotten logs, which turns them into soil faster.

Lots of animals benefit from the things Sorya does!

SORYA WAS HAPPIER NOW, IN HER NEW HOME.

SUN BEARS ARE ALSO CALLED "HONEY BEARS" BECAUSE THEY'RE GOOD AT CLIMBING TREES AND USE THEIR STRONG SENSE OF SMELL TO LOCATE HONEY.

SORYA WAS A TRUE HONEY BEAR NOW, FINDING FOOD ALL BY HERSELF!

AT NIGHT SHE USED TO FIND ME,

AND WE'D SLEEP UNDER THE STARS.

But now, my dear Sorya is a lot more confident.

She makes her own nest in the trees and sleeps there by herself.

89

She doesn't depend on me like she used to.

But even after living by herself for some time, she'll come by to say hello.

She's learned to stay away from other humans, though.

So I know she'll stay away from poachers.

CHAPTER EIGHT

ONE MORNING, AFTER MONTHS
OF NO TROUBLE...

SORYA'S
TRACKER FELL
OFF.

AFTER SEARCHING HIGH AND LOW, I FOUND A SUN-BEAR SIGN-- CLAW MARKS IN A NEARBY TREE!

BUT THE MARKS WERE NOT SORYA'S. THIS BEAR WAS MUCH TALLER THAN HER.

THIS IS A FRESH MARK.

I STARTED TO GET WORRIED!

WHAT IF SORYA HAD WANDERED INTO ANOTHER BEAR'S TERRITORY?

WHAT IF SHE WAS ATTACKED BY AN EVEN BIGGER BEAR?

GRRR!

SORYA?!

AT FIRST THEY WERE CAUTIOUS OF EACH OTHER, AND ATE AS MANY FIGS AS THEY COULD WITHOUT MAKING EYE CONTACT.

IT WAS ALMOST LIKE THEY WERE IN AN EATING CONTEST!

BUT AFTER A WHILE, THEIR LOVE OF FOOD OVERCAME THEIR FEAR OF EACH OTHER.

CHAPTER NINE

AFTER THE FEAST, SORYA AND HER NEW FRIEND FELL ASLEEP UNDER THE FIG TREE.

THAT'S WHEN I REALIZED...

IT WAS TIME TO SAY GOODBYE TO SORYA.

BUT IT WAS HARD TO WALK AWAY.

I WANTED TO LOOK AT MY SWEET GIRL FOR A LITTLE LONGER.

CRUNCH
CRUNCH

GRRR

GRRR

GRRR

GOODBYE,
SORYA.

MY NAME IS CHANG.

I AM A WILDLIFE CONSERVATIONIST.

MY GOAL WAS TO FIND SORYA
A HOME IN THE FOREST
WHERE SHE COULD LIVE . . .

WILD AND FREE.

THE END

A MESSAGE FROM TRANG AND JEET:

WE WOULD LIKE TO SEND OUR SINCERE
THANKS TO MATT HUNT, BRIAN CRUDGE,
MARION SCHNEIDER, AND "FREE THE BEARS"
ORGANIZATION, WHO GAVE US A WONDERFUL
OPPORTUNITY TO CREATE THIS BOOK. PLEASE
VISIT "FREE THE BEARS" RESCUE CENTER IN
CAT TIEN NATIONAL PARK, VIETNAM, AND
SUPPORT THEIR WORK!

FREE
THE
BEARS

WWW.FREETHEBEARS.ORG

ILLUSTRATOR'S NOTE:

I WOULD LIKE TO THANK TRANG NGUYEN, THE BRAVE AND KIND-HEARTED CONSERVATIONIST, A FRIEND OF MINE. I WOULD NOT HAVE BEEN ABLE TO CREATE THIS WORK WITHOUT HER STORIES, HER KNOWLEDGE, AND HER REAL-LIFE EXPERIENCES. THANKS TO TRANG, I HAD THE CHANCE TO VOLUNTEER AT WILDLIFE RESCUE CENTERS AND DO FIELDWORK (THANKS MATT HUNT FOR SUPPORTING ME EVEN THOUGH WE'VE NEVER HAD THE CHANCE TO MEET). I SINCERELY APPRECIATE BRIAN CRUDGE AND MARION SCHNEIDER, THE TWO EXPERTS ON BEARS WHO SHARED THEIR VALUABLE KNOWLEDGE OF BEAR CONSERVATION. IT WAS A PRIVILEGE TO WORK WITH THEM. I WOULD ALSO LIKE TO THANK THE STAFF AND VOLUNTEERS AT "FREE THE BEARS" RESCUE CENTER IN CAT TIEN NATIONAL PARK, VIETNAM, AND PHNOM TAMAO WILDLIFE RESCUE CENTER IN CAMBODIA.

MY GRATITUDE GOES TO PHUONG AN (PAN) AND NGUYET HANG (MOCHI MUN), MY TWO LOVELY AND DEDICATED ASSISTANTS. BESIDE THE HARD WORK OF SEARCHING, CATEGORIZING, DRAWING, AND TAKING DETAILED NOTES ON PLANTS ENDEMIC TO VIETNAM, THEY ALSO PROVIDED ME WITH DRAWING PAPER AND FOOD WHEN TIMES WERE TOUGH.

THANKS TO TA LAN HANH FOR INTRODUCING ME TO LINH PHAN, THE TALENTED DESIGNER WHO WAS FULLY DEVOTED TO THE PROJECT.

AND ONCE AGAIN, THANKS TRANG, FOR YOUR PATIENCE.

JEET ZDUNG

ABOUT THE CREATORS:

TRANG NGUYEN IS A VIETNAMESE WILDLIFE CONSERVATIONIST, ENVIRONMENTAL ACTIVIST, AND WRITER, KNOWN FOR HER CONSERVATION WORK IN TACKLING THE ILLEGAL WILDLIFE TRADE IN AFRICA AND ASIA. TRANG GRADUATED WITH HER PHD IN BIODIVERSITY MANAGEMENT AT THE UNIVERSITY OF KENT, ENGLAND, RESEARCHING WILD ANIMAL PART USE IN TRADITIONAL ASIAN MEDICINE AND ITS IMPACT ON AFRICAN WILDLIFE. IN 2018, TRANG WAS FEATURED IN THE DOCUMENTARY FILM *STROOP: JOURNEY INTO THE RHINO HORN WAR,* ALONGSIDE JANE GOODALL. SHE WAS SELECTED BY BBC FOR THEIR 100 WOMEN OF 2019 LIST AND BY FORBES FOR THEIR 2020 30 UNDER 30 ASIA LIST. TRANG IS THE FOUNDER AND EXECUTIVE DIRECTOR OF WILDACT, AN NGO THAT MONITORS THE ILLEGAL WILDLIFE TRADE MARKETS AND PROVIDES CONSERVATION EDUCATION PROGRAMS FOR VIETNAMESE YOUTH. SHE IS ALSO A MEMBER OF THE IUCN SSC BEAR SPECIALIST GROUP, WHICH STRIVES TO PROMOTE THE CONSERVATION OF BEARS LIVING IN THEIR NATURAL HABITATS AROUND THE WORLD. *SAVING SORYA: CHANG AND THE SUN BEAR* IS HER FIRST CHILDREN'S BOOK.

JEET ZDUNG IS AN ILLUSTRATOR WHO FUSES TRADITIONAL VIETNAMESE ART WITH MANGA, USING PENCILS, WATERCOLORS, INK, AND OTHER DIGITAL MEANS TO CREATE WORKS OF BEAUTY AND INNOVATION. HE HAS WON SEVERAL AWARDS, INCLUDING A SILENT MANGA AUDITION EXCELLENCE AWARD FOR HIS MANGA *STAND UP AND FLY. SAVING SORYA: CHANG AND THE SUN BEAR* IS HIS FIRST CHILDREN'S BOOK PUBLISHED IN THE US. HE LIVES IN HANOI, VIETNAM.

WILDACT IS A NOT-FOR-PROFIT CONSERVATION ORGANIZATION BASED IN VIETNAM, ESTABLISHED IN 2015. ITS MISSION IS TO INSPIRE, MOTIVATE, AND EMPOWER SOCIETY AND INDIVIDUALS TO ENGAGE IN THE SCIENCE-BASED CONSERVATION OF THREATENED SPECIES AND ECOSYSTEMS.

WildAct

DIAL BOOKS FOR YOUNG READERS
AN IMPRINT OF PENGUIN RANDOM HOUSE LLC, NEW YORK

ORIGINALLY PUBLISHED IN VIETNAMESE AS *CHANG HOANG DÃ – GẤU* BY KIM DONG PUBLISHING COMPANY, 2020.
FIRST ENGLISH LANGUAGE PUBLICATION IN THE UNITED KINGDOM BY MACMILLAN CHILDREN'S BOOKS, AN IMPRINT OF PAN MACMILLAN, 2021

ORIGINAL TEXT COPYRIGHT © 2020 BY TRANG NGUYEN
TRANSLATION COPYRIGHT © 2021 BY TRANG NGUYEN
ILLUSTRATIONS COPYRIGHT © 2020 BY JEET ZDUNG

VISIT US ONLINE AT PENGUINRANDOMHOUSE.COM.

FIRST AMERICAN EDITION
LIBRARY OF CONGRESS CATALOGING-IN-PUBLICATION DATA IS AVAILABLE.
MANUFACTURED IN CHINA
ISBN 9780593353639 HC   10 9 8 7 6 5 4 3 2 1
ISBN 9780593353622 PB   10 9 8 7 6 5 4 3 2 1

TEXT SET IN DAN PANOSIAN, JACK ARMSTRONG, AND TWO FISTED